Ou

Roderick Hunt • Alex Brychta

OXFORD

UNIVERSITY PRESS

Floppy was dreaming that
he was in the desert.

It was hot in the desert.

The sand was hot.
"Ouch!" said Floppy.

Floppy saw a girl on a horse.

The girl was Biff!

"Quick! Come with me,"
said Biff.

"A sandstorm is coming."

The wind blew the sand.

Biff put Floppy on the horse.

The horse went fast.

"Go faster!" said Biff.

"The sandstorm is coming!"

The horse went faster.

"Ouch!" said Floppy.

The horse stopped.
Oh no!

Floppy flew off the horse.

"Ouch!" said Floppy.

"Oh! There's my cactus,"
said Biff.

Think about the story

Why do you think
this story is called
'Ouch!'?

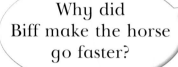

Why did
Biff make the horse
go faster?

Why isn't
it a good idea
to touch a cactus?

What do
you dream
about?

Picture puzzle

How many things can you find beginning with the
same sound as the 'c' in cat?

**Useful common words repeated in this story and
other books at Level 2.**

coming   fast   girl   said   the   was   went

Names: Biff   Floppy

(Answer to picture puzzle: cactus, cake, candle, car, carrot, cat, caterpillar, cup)